Sarah's Brave Adventure

A YOGA JOURNEY

This book is for you!
May you find strength, balance, and confidence to make every day an adventure—Cosmic Kids

PENGUIN YOUNG READERS LICENSES
An imprint of Penguin Random House LLC, New York

First published in the United States of America by Penguin Young Readers Licenses,
an imprint of Penguin Random House LLC, New York, 2022

Visit us online at penguinrandomhouse.com.

Manufactured in China

ISBN 9780593386279   10 9 8 7 6 5 4 3 2 1 HH

Design by Taylor Abatiell

COSMIC KIDS!

Sarah's Brave Adventure

A YOGA JOURNEY

by Brooke Vitale
illustrated by Junissa Bianda

Sarah opened her eyes and grinned. Morning was her favorite time of day. Each new sunrise meant the chance for new adventures.

Hopping out of bed, Sarah stretched her arms to the sky. She bent over and stretched her back. Finally, she stood and moved to the window.

"Good morning, **SUN**," she said. "What do you have in store for me today?"

Sarah swung open her **door**, then stopped.

Lying on the floor was an envelope with her name on it.

For me? Sarah wondered.

Curious, she tore it open. Inside was a note!

Sarah looked around, excited. She wondered who had left the note for her.

"I guess I'll find out soon enough," she said.

And without wasting another minute, she set out toward the trees that separated her home from the mountain.

Sarah pushed on through the forest. But the farther she went, the closer together the **trees** grew. Soon, they blocked out the sun completely.

Sarah shivered in the dark forest, wishing she'd brought a light. Shadows crept between the trees, and each crackling branch made her jump. Looking over her shoulder, she wondered if she should turn back.

Suddenly, something brushed past Sarah's leg.

"Agh!" she screamed.

At Sarah's feet, a **cat** meowed. Sarah laughed. She couldn't believe she'd been scared of a *cat*!

Bending down, she petted the cat. "I bet you don't have any trouble seeing in here, do you? I wish I were more like you. If I could see in the dark, maybe I wouldn't be so afraid."

The cat meowed again and stretched its back.
"You're right," Sarah said. "The trees have to
end eventually. I just need to keep going."

Taking a deep breath, Sarah pushed on.

Soon, she heard the sound of rushing water. The trees cleared to reveal a river. A **turtle** lazily paddled past her.

Sarah's heart pounded in her chest. "I wish I could be like you, turtle," she said. "Then I could swim across the river!"

But Sarah knew that wasn't a choice. She didn't know *how* to swim. She'd have to find another way.

Sarah looked around. Behind her, she spied a long, heavy log.

That's it, she thought. *I'll make a* **bridge**.

Little by little, Sarah heaved the log toward the river. And little by little, she shoved it across the water. Finally, her bridge was ready.

It wasn't perfect, but it would have to do.

Setting one foot on the log, she began to walk across it.

"Ha!" Sarah shouted as she jumped off the log and onto the opposite bank. "I did it!"

Waving goodbye to the turtle, Sarah kept moving.

A few minutes later, she found herself in a field of flowers. A **butterfly** flew past her nose, and she stopped to look at it.

"You are so beautiful, butterfly," Sarah said, enjoying the view. "And your home is so beautiful, too! I wish I could stay here forever."

As Sarah watched the butterfly flap away, she had an idea. Bending, she plucked a single **flower** from the field. "There," she said, tucking it behind her ear. "Now I have a piece of this beautiful garden to remind me of this place!"

Pushing her way through the flowers, Sarah reached the base of the **mountain**.

She tipped her head back . . . and back . . . and back.

The top of the mountain was so high up. How was she ever going to get up there?

Overhead, an **eagle** soared by. "I wish I were like you, eagle," Sarah said. "Then I could fly to the top of the mountain. But instead I'm stuck down here!"

Sarah shook her head. There was no use wishing, She couldn't fly, and that was that. Which left only one option: She'd have to **climb**.

One foot above the other and one hand above the other, Sarah slowly made her way up the mountain.

Finally, she got to the very top of the mountain! Exhausted, she felt like she could sleep for the rest of the day!

Then, out of the corner of her eye, Sarah spied a small **house**. That must be where she was meant to go.

I wonder what's waiting inside, she thought.

Curious, Sarah opened the front door.

"Surprise!" several voices cried out.

Sarah gasped. A party for *her*?

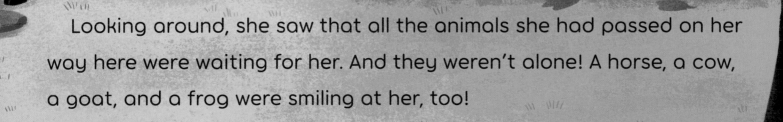

Looking around, she saw that all the animals she had passed on her way here were waiting for her. And they weren't alone! A horse, a cow, a goat, and a frog were smiling at her, too!

Sarah grinned. She was so happy to see her animal friends. But she was confused, too.

"Why would you throw a party for . . . *me*?" she asked. "I'm nothing special."

"Oh, but you are," the eagle replied. "You are brave and strong and resourceful. Without those traits, you never would have made it up the mountain. You are our **hero**."

Pulling up a **chair**, Sarah thought about her journey.

They were right.

She had been brave in the dark forest.

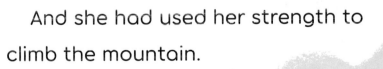

She had used her wits to find a way across the river.

And she had used her strength to climb the mountain.

Maybe she *was* special, after all.

With a big grin, Sarah stood up. One by one, she hugged each of her friends.

"Thank you," she said. "For making me see the truth. Now . . . who's ready for a party!"